LORD OF THE BEARS

Sandy

Cobby

Philpot

Pebbles

The Bear Facts

Alice in Bearland

For Paddy, Tom,
Jack, and Leon.

First published in 2004 by The Bear Shop Book Co.,
an imprint of Emma Treehouse Ltd.,
Old Brewhouse, Shepton Mallet BA4 5QE
ISBN 1 85576 416 4
Printed in China
2 4 6 8 10 9 7 5 3 1

Sandy

Paints a Picture

Rikey Austin

The Bear Shop Book Co.

Alice's Bear Shop was in a small town. Children (and grown-ups) from miles around brought sick and hurt bears to Alice's Bear Shop, knowing that Alice would make them better. This was because when Alice talked to bears, the bears talked back.

Many people lived and worked in the town, and many came to visit, because it was such a beautiful place and because it was beside the ocean.

One of the people who worked in the town was an artist. The artist lived just around the corner from Alice's Bear Shop with a teddy bear called Sandy. The artist painted beautiful pictures of all kinds of things, and whenever someone came to buy one of her paintings, Sandy could see that the pictures made them smile.

"I wish I could make someone smile like that," she thought.

On one particular day the artist was working in her studio when she suddenly brushed the hair from her face, dropped her paintbrush into a jar of murky water, and stretched her aching back. She had been painting for many hours. She was very tired and a little sad, because her painting was not going as well as she wanted.

"I think I'll go for a walk along the beach and blow the cobwebs away," she told Sandy.

"I wish I could make her smile,"
thought Sandy, "like she makes the people
who see her paintings smile."

Outside, the sun was shining and the wind was blowing across the beach, whipping the little waves up into foam as they hurried across the sand. The artist took a deep breath of fresh sea air. Seeing all the other people on the beach enjoying themselves made her feel better.

In the studio Sandy had made a plan.

"I'll paint her a picture," she said to herself. "I've seen it done so many times, how hard can it be?" She got a blank canvas to paint on from the stack by the wall and struggled to push it up onto the rickety trestle table where the artist kept her brushes and paints.

Sandy clambered up
a tall stool to sit beside it.
There were all the paints
and the artist's palette,
covered in all kinds of
colors, laid out
before her.

"Oh, look at all the colors," said Sandy, getting more excited by her plan all the time. Impatient to start, she grabbed the brightest colors she could find.

"Red's nice," she said, and gave the tube a big squeeze. Paint squirted up into the air. Splat! A big blob landed on the front of her dress.

"Oh!" said Sandy. She looked down in surprise and stepped back, knocking the jar of murky water over.

"Oh, oh!" said Sandy, turning around.

She slipped in the spilled water and sat down with a bump.

"Oh, oh, oh!" said Sandy, just before tumbling head-over-heels off the edge of the table.

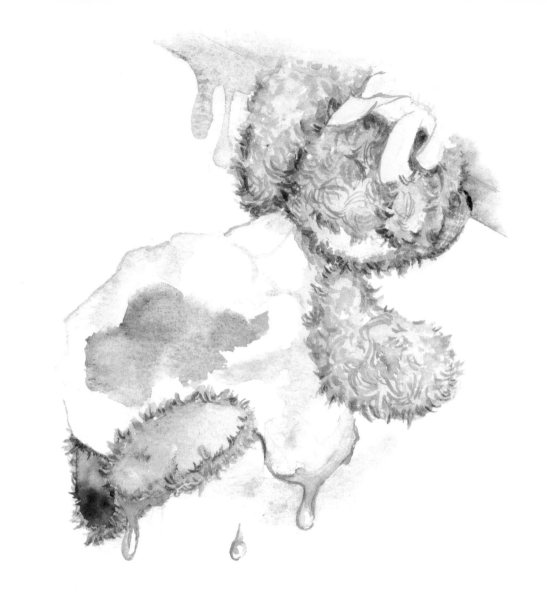

She grabbed at the wobbly tabletop to stop herself from falling.

"Oh, oh, oh, oh!" said Sandy, as very slowly the whole tabletop tilted up and slipped gracefully to the floor with Sandy still hanging on.

Paints, water, and brushes all slid with a crash on top of her.

As the last paintbrush rolled to a stop, the door opened. The artist stood in the doorway with her mouth hanging open and her eyes as wide as saucers.

Sandy looked up sadly. She was covered from head to foot in paint but hadn't managed to get even a single brush mark on the canvas.

"Well, look at you!" said the artist. "We'd better get Alice to clean you up."

She carried the sad little bear around the corner to Alice's Bear Shop and handed her over to Alice.

"My worktable collapsed when I was out," explained the artist. "I keep meaning to get it fixed. Poor Sandy must have been underneath. Can you clean her up?"

Bears
cared for
and
repaired.

Alice said that she could.
The artist excused herself and dashed off,
saying "I'm sorry to rush out, but I need to
clean up the gallery and there's a painting
that I'd really like to get done."

Sandy was worried that the artist, whom
she loved very much, might be angry.

So as Alice gently sponged away the
the paint from her fur and dress, Sandy
explained her plan and how it had gone so
wrong. "That was a lovely idea," said Alice.

"Yes," agreed Sandy, "but it didn't work.
All I have done is make her more
sad and angry."

"Oh, I don't know," said Alice.
"I think your artist was excited about a plan
of her own when she rushed off.
Every cloud has a silver lining!"

When Sandy was cleaned up Alice carried her back to the gallery.

Everything was back in its place, and the artist was busy on a painting.

Then the artist moved back proudly, and Sandy could see what she had been painting. Sandy could not believe her eyes. There was a beautiful painting of her, her fur and dress covered in bright splashes of color.

"She looked so funny covered in paint," the artist laughed, "I had to paint this picture. I am going to hang it here on the wall. Do you like it?" she asked Alice.

"I think it is wonderful," said Alice.

"I do too," said the artist. "I can't help smiling every time I look at it."

Paws for Thought!
by Ted E. Bear
The Thirty-Nine Bears
Seven Brides for Seven Bears
Tat
Woodroffe
BEAR HEROES
Cooking for Single Bears by Julia Bear
Ting
Icky
Mary-Jane